Brave Magic

Other brilliant stories to collect:

Brave
Magic

Retold by
Geraldine McCaughrean

Illustrated by
Cathie Felstead

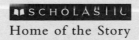
Home of the Story

For Natasha and Toby Fox

Scholastic Children's Books,
Commonwealth House, 1–19 New Oxford Street,
London WC1A 1NU, UK
a division of Scholastic Ltd
London ~ New York ~ Toronto ~ Sydney ~ Auckland
Mexico City ~ New Delhi ~ Hong Kong

First published by Scholastic Ltd, 1999

ISBN 0 439 01141 8

Printed by Cox and Wyman Ltd, Reading, Berks.

4 6 8 10 9 7 5 3

Chapter One
TWIN OPPOSITES

Who was the fool who said that two people born at the same time, under the same array of stars will be alike? Glooscap and Malsum were born within moments of each other — and of the same mother, too — but

there were never two men more different. Everything about Glooscap was beautiful, from the smooth insides of his wrists to the colours of his dreams. Everything about Malsum was ugly, from his acid yellow eyes to the mischief he kept in his mittens.

When they were born, there was little more to the world than pine trees and a sprinkling of stars overhead.

Glooscap looked around him and wondered how he could make life easier for the people and animals living there. So he created flat, sunny meadows, sweetcorn and maple syrup, medicinal herbs and moose-hide string, holidays, apple trees and fur coats for the bears.

Malsum, on the other hand, looked around him and wondered what he

could do to make life more difficult. So he created cacti and leeches, poison berries and rattlesnakes, cliffs, deserts and Monday mornings, witch-craft and sorcery.

Worst of all his mischief he saved for his brother. For Malsum longed to *kill* Glooscap, and though they had both been born to live for several thousand years, Malsum knew there *was* a

way of killing him, if only he could discover the secret.

"I have to admit," he said one day, "I've been mortally afraid of ferns ever since Mother told me that the fern-root could be the death of me." Then he smiled a sickly smile. "Surely nothing could kill *you*, though, brother dear? Not the glorious Glooscap?"

"It's owl feathers with me," said Glooscap, and marvelled at the speed with which his brother hurried away.

Malsum went at once and found his bow. At dusk, he shot an owl out of a

tree and rent a bunch of feathers out of its limp little body. Creeping up behind his brother, he broke the feathers over his head.

Instantly, Glooscap fell dead.

Malsum stood holding the drooping feathers, his jaw hanging open in delight, his tongue dangling. It had been so easy! Now he was lord of all Nature, and could sow crows in the

cornfields, thistles in the clearings, gnats in the sunny places.

First, to make absolutely sure Glooscap was dead, Malsum slunk closer. The hands were still. The eyelids did not flicker. He would just hold his cheek close to the lips, to feel for signs of breathing...

As he did so, Glooscap sneezed directly down his ear, yawned and

sat up. Although he was gentle and peacable, Glooscap was far from stupid. "I said an owl's feather would kill me. I didn't say anything about staying dead," he pointed out.

Malsum hid the owl feathers behind his back and pretended not to understand.

But he went straight to Beaver's holt and asked a favour. "Sister Beaver, listen and eavesdrop and spy. Find out what can kill my brother lastingly dead, and I shall grant you any wish!"

So all that summer, whenever Glooscap sat on a river bank to cool his feet or to watch the fish, Beaver would be close by, cruising through the water, leaving her silver wake behind her, leaving her ears above water to catch every word Glooscap spoke. She became so familiar a sight that Glooscap would call out, "Hello again, old friend! Good to see you!"

And they struck up such a friend-
ship that Beaver forgot all about her
deal with Malsum.

Almost.

One day she invited Glooscap to wade
out through the reeds and inspect her
new dam. "I would love to," said
Glooscap, "but the reeds are in flower,
and the flowering reed is the only
thing on this beautiful earth which

can do me lasting harm."

At once Beaver knew that she could have her wish. And it was a wish so dear to her — a life-long wish — that she went at once to Malsum with what she knew. "Now! My wish! Please grant me wings like a pigeon, Malsum! I've always longed to soar in the sky and see my reflection below me in the great lake and to pillow my head on the clouds!"

At the thought of fat little Beaver flying about in the treetops, Malsum rolled on his back in the grass and laughed till tears ran from his acid

yellow eyes. "*You*, you disappointed doormat? Tail like a moose-pat? Teeth like a rabbit? You want *wings*? Why would you want to look more ridiculous than you already do?"

Beaver, wounded to the heart, her dreams grounded in the mud, instantly regretted betraying her friend. Her little head cut a path as fast as a speeding silver arrow

across the lake's surface. "Glooscap! Oh Glooscap! I have done a terrible thing!" she wept. "I have betrayed your secret to your brother, and now he is coming to … ah!" She broke off in horror, as, on the bank behind Glooscap loomed up the shape of Malsum wielding a flowering reed like a javelin.

Forewarned, Glooscap rolled aside into a clump of ferns; the reed glanced across his shoulder and fell harmlessly into the lake. Glooscap, spread-eagled on the ground, found his hand closing around a fern-root.

Then and there, he could have struck his brother dead. He was angry enough. He would have been justified. But when the fern root struck Malsum, it knocked him on to all-fours, yes. It put an end to his mischief, yes. But it did not kill him. His yellow eyes were still alive with hatred. His tongue still hung out, ravenous for death. But now he was as

shaggy as any bear, black as any panther, and held prisoner by the power of Glooscap's magic.

Ever afterwards, wherever Glooscap went, he was accompanied by two birds who flew about the world and brought him the news, good and bad. At his thigh, too, ran a great black wolf, doing his bidding despite itself, doing good despite its evil nature.

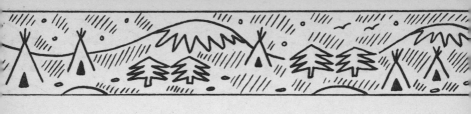

Chapter Two
THE BIGGER MAGIC

There was a lot to be done to put right all the evil Malsum had begun. Every night, witches circled in the sky like bats, and magicians squatted like toads beside every waterhole.

To help him in his work, Glooscap

took his penknife and peeled the bark from the ash trees in little curling strips. As these shavings fell to the ground, they came to life – as elves, brittle and silvery as the bark itself, with knotty hands and eyes like tree-amber – helpers for the task of finishing the world.

They swept up the witches like windfall crab-apples. They sluiced away

the magicians like so many rabbit droppings. At last only one sorceror remained; unfortunately, he was more wicked than all the rest rolled together.

"Your time is past," said Glooscap to Win-pe. "Go away."

"Make me," said Win-pe, and began to grow.

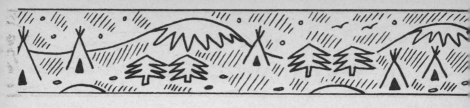

Now Glooscap stood as tall as any sunflower. But Win-pe pulled himself up to the height of a tree. Peering down at Glooscap's parting and top-knot of feathers, Win-pe began to laugh, and the larger he grew, the larger his laugh, until the noise broke down Beaver's dam, cracked Eagle's eggs, sent avalanches hurtling down the mountainsides.

Win-pe grew until Glooscap was no taller than his thigh, no taller than his knee, no taller than the arch of his foot. Then he lifted that foot and said, "Watch, World, while I squash your beloved Glooscap like a white wasp under my boot!"

"Beware, Win-pe!" Glooscap replied. "The wasp may sting you!" Then he held one finger in the air.

That finger reached above Win-pe's instep, reached above his ankle bone, in fact. Glooscap too was growing — and at such a speed that he seemed to rocket out of the ground like a

hot-water geyser. His head passed the treetops and the hills, scattered flocks of birds and emptied the clouds of their rain.

Momentarily, the two giants stood face-to-face, both head-high to the mountain tops. But Glooscap was still growing!

At last his shoulders were wrapped in the Milky Way, and the dog star

glinted in his eye. Glooscap lifted his knuckles and knocked — oh so very gently — on Win-pe's forehead.

What with the surprise, what with leaning over backwards to gape up at Glooscap, the knock was just enough to unbalance Win-pe.

If he had been only as tall as a sunflower or a hogan, only as tall as a teepee or a tree, he might have

fallen without hurting himself. But Win-pe was as tall as a mountain, and when mountains fall, they make a substantial mess.

Win-pe broke into a million boulders, flints and pebbles, and his laugh fell in the streams and rivers, who immediately put it to good use. Now every time you hear a stream giggle or a river over-brimming with gurgling

laughter, it is because the water has remembered the downfall of Win-pe at the hands of glorious Glooscap.

Chapter Three
FETCHING SUMMER

Now I think of it, there was one giant, too, who got the better of Glooscap for a while. He lived in the north, and was not the axe-wielding, ambushing, blood-thirsty, bone-crunching kind of giant. On the

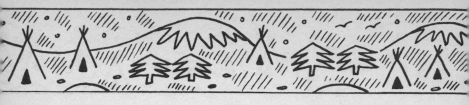

contrary, he would always greet any passing hedgehog or bear or trapper most courteously and invite them into his teepee.

Once supper was eaten and the pipe-of-friendship lit, Old Man Winter would begin his storytelling. And the sing-song lilt of his low, low voice and the blue-hazy maze of coiling smoke rings would lull and

lullaby the visitor to sleep – for whole days and weeks and months at a time. Some never woke again in all their lives.

Even Glooscap was not immune to the magic. As he strode past the white teepee one day, wolf at his heels and birds about his head, Old Man Winter called out to him. Unsuspecting, he ducked inside.

Supper was good. While the stories rose and fell like a field of windblown summer grass, and the tobacco smoke muzzed his mind, Glooscap struggled to stay awake, but his chin soon sank on to his chest and he was asleep.

For months he slept, until a glimmer of magic, small as a glowing ember, pricked him awake. Coughing and wiping his eyes, he crawled

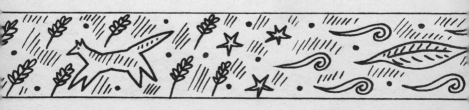

outside ... only to find the whole land transformed! The ground was covered by soft snow and sharp ice, the lakes were frozen, and the trees were a-clatter with icicles. His wolf companion sat howling, its black fur dusted with frost.

All the people and animals were shivering cold. And the birds were silent.

Glooscap's own hands were so cold that he could not work any magic to dispel this dreadful, chilling whiteness. So he wandered about, worried and helpless, his feet blue inside his moccasins, until he turned south and reached a land free of snow.

The sound of music drew him deep into a vast forest. Treading so softly that his moccasins left no prints,

he padded in search of the music-makers. In a clearing at the centre of the forest, he found them: a group of tiny people dancing to the music of chirruping crickets.

They were cloaked in such brightness that they looked like fragments of light glancing off windblown water.

Worming his way forwards on his stomach, Glooscap crept closer, closer

still. There, in among the dancers, was one tiny woman more beautiful than all the rest, with dragonfly wings, a pelt of pollen, and with thistledown hair. The others called her "Queen Summer".

Coiling his legs up under him, Glooscap sprang forward! His reaching hand closed round the woman — she flickered inside his grasp like a

butterfly — and he quickly tied the tip of his lasso around her waist. Then he set her free to flutter down from his hands. But she was only as free as a fish on the end of a line — free to run after him wherever he ran.

The Elves of Light rushed to her rescue, trying to unfasten the knot, but Glooscap was away and running, trailing the woman behind him, to coax the elves after him. Uphill and down canyon he led them, Queen Summer glimmering like a fishing lure on an evening river.

Northwards, all the time northwards,

Glooscap led his clamouring troupe of elves, until they reached the frost-tinkling reeds of the frozen north country, those trees clump-haired with snow, those drifts of muffling whiteness.

Wherever Queen Summer and the elves set foot, the cold lost its grip. The ice became transparent, then liquid. Colours came back to the countryside as to a face recovering

from illness. The animals gorged on grass they had not seen for six months, and the people wrung the slush out of their mocassins and danced barefoot on drifts of flowers.

At last Glooscap picked up Queen Summer again in the palm of his hand and, hiding her inside his coat, went to the teepee of Old Man Winter.

Once again he was welcomed with

the offer of supper, a smoke and a story. Once again the soothing, somnambulant murmurings of the Old Man's magic began to lull and lullaby Glooscap to sleep...

But then the story faltered. Old Man's face was pink. Without realizing it, he was sensing the presence in his home of Queen Summer. He fanned himself, finding his bitter tent uncomfortably, inexplicably warm. "I'm sorry. Where was I?" he mumbled and, taking a sip of water, unfastened his white shirt. Sweat began to pour down his

face, and he tottered to his feet. "I regret … air … I must just step outside."

But before Old Man Winter could reach the flap of his teepee, both he and the teepee began to melt. Like a snowman in the glare of July, Old Man Winter succumbed to Queen Summer, and all around his tent the birds suddenly burst out singing.

Glooscap set Queen Summer free and thanked her. And to the music of birdsong, she and her Elves of Light danced splashily southwards through the thaw. Taking a slow and round-about way home, it was months before they were hidden away once more in the heart of their southerly forest home.

Sadly, Old Man Winter has many brothers. Once a year, a teepee appears deep in the glades of Glooscap's territory and the white magic begins all over again. Once a year Queen Summer must be fetched or lured from her distant realm, and make the long journey north, to restore the colours and the birdsong. And while the white world waits, a black wolf howls, his fur powdered with frost.

Chapter Four

THE UNCONQUERABLE WASIM

The giants had packed up their buffalo-hide bags and left for ever. The magicians had all disappeared in a puff of smoke. Wicked Malsum had been turned into a wolf; even grim Pamola, who haunted the primeval

dark, had dissolved away like a bad dream.

Glooscap looked round him with satisfaction, brushed the palms of his hands together and grinned. "I don't believe there is anyone left for me to conquer."

"Oho, is that so?" said his wife, hoeing her vegetable patch. "I know one tyrant you won't tame, for all

your magic!" and she laughed (though only to herself).

"Who? *Who*, woman? Take me to him! Let me look him in the eyes!" declared Glooscap, nettled by her laughter.

To his surprise, she simply took him indoors, removing the brow band from her forehead as she went, laying down the cradle-board in which she carried

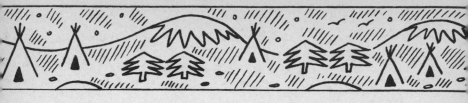

their son about with her while she
worked. She lifted out the baby,
Wasim, and sat him on the floor with
a lump of maple sugar to suck. "Call
him to you," she said to her husband.

"Who? Wasim?"

"The baby. Yes."

So Glooscap, still bewildered, called
out to his baby son: "Come here."

The baby looked round, but
continued to sit sucking his maple
sugar.

"I said, *come here*," said Glooscap
firmly.

"Goo," said Wasim.

"Your father has spoken. It is your duty to obey!" snapped Glooscap.

"Goo goo," said Wasim.

"*I summon thee this instant!*" demanded Glooscap pompously.

"Ahugh goo," said Wasim.

"*Get yourself over here!*" bellowed Glooscap, but the baby only burst into tears, crawled in the opposite direction and began tugging the black wolf's tail.

Well, after that Glooscap sang. He stood on his head and recited spells. He danced a powerful dance … but all that happened was that it started to rain indoors.

He turned himself into a songbird and warbled merrily for half an hour. At least Wasim stirred himself to cross the floor… But only so as to pull a yellow feather out of the bird's tail. Glooscap quickly changed back into his own shape, rubbing his bottom and muttering.

He made such magic that the dead sat up in their graves and complained

about the noise. But Wasim only gig-
gled and dribbled and bubbled and
burbled: "A-goo-goo-goo."

At last Glooscap, his plaits all
unwound, his laces all undone,
shedding head-feathers like a
moulting chicken, stormed out of the
house and rampaged about the forests,
making a terrible din. It was only the
pine cones falling on his head which

brought him to his senses.

Then he saw how the birds were sitting – open-beaked, trembling. The squirrels were staring at him, their tails erect behind them like so many question marks, as if to say, "What's the matter? What's the matter? What's the matter?"

With one last bad-tempered stamp of his foot, Glooscap ducked his head

between his shoulders and grunted,
"Nothing. It's nothing at all. Don't
worry about it. Nothing to worry
about." And back he went to admit
defeat.

"You win, you win!" he called to his
wife from the doorway. "There *is* one
tyrant in the world I can never
vanquish!" He gave a chuckle, then a
snort. Then he put his hands on his

hips and began to laugh out loud.

Wasim looked up, gave a hiccup of joy at hearing his father laughing, and went to get a cuddle. "A-gloo-gloo," he said affectionately.

So says each and every baby when, remembering the triumph of Wasim over his father, he attempts to say the difficult Algonquin name of Gloo-Gloo-Glooscap.

Chapter Five
THREE FAVOURS

That was about the last time that Glooscap laughed.

Oh, the animals sometimes brought a smile to his lips — the acrobatics of the chipmunks, the bears fishing for salmon. He delighted in the dance of

the bees and the frantic hammering of the woodpecker. But when he looked at the human race ... well, he could not raise so much as a chuckle.

Mankind was forever fighting and quarrelling, setting traps for Glooscap's animals, telling lies to the trees, throwing stones at the stars. Unlike his wicked twin, Glooscap did not want to *destroy* Mankind; he just

did not want to spend thousands of years living next-door to him.

So he let it be known that he would soon be leaving. "I am going deep into the forests, far away from everything and everyone. There I shall rest for seven years. After that I shall leave the world altogether."

Everyone tried to dissuade him. Beaver, Marmot and Chipmunk said:

"Don't go! We love you! We'll miss you too much!"

Mankind said sulkily: "You obviously don't care about *us* at all."

Glooscap regarded them coldly for a moment, then said: "If any brave soul can be troubled to seek me out, I shall grant him a wish ... for old time's sake."

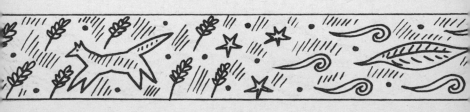

Now people being what they are, Mankind became suddenly more eager to see Glooscap than he ever had been. In return for a wish, people were ready to fight their way through briars and brambles, over hills and mountains, through the dark of night and the heat of day in order to interrupt Glooscap's peace and quiet.

But he had chosen his hideaway carefully, and most who left in search of a wish had to admit defeat and turn for home. Only three hardy individuals persevered, through hardship and difficulty, and blundered their way into the clearing where Glooscap's teepee stood, a black wolf asleep at its door.

"Master! Master!" said the first. "I

had to find you before you left! No one but you can help me!"

"What is your wish?" asked Glooscap warily.

"Not to be me! To be different, I mean! To change… To be better!"

"How, 'better'?" asked Glooscap.

The man found it hard to speak the words. He hung his head and scuffed his foot. "All my life I have had a foul temper. I've made life a misery for my wife … and now my own children are afraid of me. Oh Glooscap! You're gentle like the spring breeze. Won't you make me gentle, too?"

Glooscap reached into his wampum bag and pulled out a box. "This is the best I can do for you," he said. "Don't open it until you reach home."

As the first man ducked out through the tent flap, he cracked heads with a ragged little woman coming the other way. *"Look where you're..."* he began to say, instantly raging. But in a

desperate effort to govern his bad temper in front of gentle Glooscap, he bit his tongue and held the flap for the woman to pass.

"Oh Master! Master!" whispered the woman, launching straight into the speech she had prepared. "Don't despise me, I beg you! My clothes are ragged, but my heart is not so *very* bad, you know."

"Despise you?" said Glooscap, who had never despised anyone in his life.

"I'm a widow, you see, and have no money, no animals — not even a piece of ground to grow vegetables in...

The shame I could bear, but…"

"What is your wish?" asked Glooscap, intrigued.

"To have corn enough to feed my children, Master!" said the woman imploringly. "Life has left me too poor to keep them from starving, and my neighbours won't spare us so much as the ash from their fires."

Glooscap shook his head sadly. "It is just such unkindness that is driving me away. When did I ever begrudge them the dew in the morning or the sun in their faces?" he muttered, puzzled past patience. "And is this how they treat each other?"

He gave the woman a box from his wampum bag, but told her not to open it until she reached home.

At the edge of the clearing, she came face-to-face with a tall man decorated from head to foot in shells, beads, feathers and silver ornaments. He did not exactly look at her, but deigned to sneer a little when she had gone by. He sneered, too, at the black wolf, which growled a rumbling growl.

"Oh Glooscap! Brother!" the tall man began, before he had even entered the

lodge. "I have always thought of you and myself as kindred spirits! Alike in so many ways! Grant, therefore, that I too should stand tall and admirable, strong and beautiful among the piffling little people of my piddling little village – a giant among dwarfs!"

"Why are you limping?" asked Glooscap.

"Some moss got into my moccasins," said the man, taken aback – also a little put out that Glooscap could find nothing better to say to a kindred spirit. In fact he regularly stuffed his moccasins full of moss to make

himself look taller ... but soon he would never need to do it again! The box was already out of Glooscap's wampum bag! The vain, jingling, arrogant popinjay reached out and snatched it eagerly.

"Don't open it till you get home ... er ... brother," said Glooscap.

By the time the first, bad-tempered man got home, he was exhausted. He

just knew that when his children ran to meet him, he would say something he did not mean: something sharp or unkind; it had happened so many times before. He shook the box and, when it did not rattle, thought that Glooscap had refused his foolish wish, and threw it aside.

Perhaps it did not matter. After all, he was safe home after a terrible journey full of danger. He could see his wife standing in the door of his hogan, the youngest child in her arms. And he suddenly felt such a wave of tenderness towards them that tears of

joy ran down his face. His children ran up and flung their arms around his thighs … and he was too choked with happiness to utter one word, let alone anything sharp or unkind.

No cross word ever passed his lips again: somehow happiness got in the way every time.

And, of course, happiness doesn't rattle when you shake it.

Meanwhile, the poor widow reached her home village, kissed her skinny children, and opened her precious, hard-won box. Inside it she found a few grains of seed corn which she planted by her door. "Well, at least the dear fellow has given me more than our neighbours ever did," she told the children, with a sigh and a shrug.

Overnight, those seeds grew. They grew into seedlings, into shoots. In fact, they grew into fully grown, fully ripe corn-maize. And when the woman looked out next morning, startled by the sight of corn cobs outside her window, she found there was rather more maize than she had been expecting...

In fact her corn spread out as far as the horizon in every direction so that

her neighbours' houses looked like islands in a sea of corn. And moving amid the corn were fifty dappled horses, a hundred golden pheasants and a sprinkling of white doves.

The third person had no doubts his wish would be granted, for in his opinion he deserved no less. The moment he reached the outskirts of his village, he opened the box, and out poured its magic.

No more need to stuff moss in his moccasins. No more need to buy silver ornaments. No more need to tire himself saying, "Hey, look at me!

Aren't I fine? Aren't I the bee's knees?"

No, there was no one so tall in the whole village; no one so stately, dignified or beautiful. For the vain man had put down roots, put out branches, sprouted twigs and was sporting needles by the million. He had turned into the tallest pine in the entire forest, and the people were

very glad of him when the songbirds sang in his hair every morning.

To tell the truth, they were more glad of him than they had ever been previously.

Chapter Six
A Great Loss

Seven years passed. On the shores of Lake Minas, Glooscap and his son loaded their white canoe with food enough for a long journey. They sang as they did so. They sang as they pushed the little boat out from the

shore, Glooscap's wife seated in the prow.

All the animals, who had gathered to say goodbye, strained to catch that sweet sound as it moved farther away over the lake. The Master had given them a great feast of farewell before going – had stroked them all and scratched each one between the ears (which is all the blessing any animal

asks), and now he was gone.

They wept at the very thought of it.

Even the black wolf put back his head and howled.

"It is only until the Golden Age," said Fox to Coyote. "Only until Mankind has learned to deserve him."

But Coyote only boggled at Fox, not understanding. And when Heron whistled or Frog croaked, when Dog

barked and Horse neighed, the sounds had no meaning for the other animals. Their common language had fallen away, like leaves in autumn, and they fled each other, unable to trust any longer in the brotherhood of beasts.

One day, one day when Glooscap returns — when his canoe comes gliding back over the water of Lake Minas — the animals will gather on the

shore to greet him, and the song of welcome they sing will be sung in just one language we all understand.

Until then, we must get by as best we can, trying to understand one another.

Other stories to collect:

Aesop's Fables

Malorie Blackman
Illustrated by Patrice Aggs

Once upon a time there was a man named Aesop
who told stories full of wisdom…

Hansel and Gretel

Henrietta Branford
Illustrated by Lesley Harker

Once upon a time there were a brother and sister
who were left alone in the forest…

The Snow Queen

Berlie Doherty
Illustrated by Siân Bailey

Once upon a time there was a little boy whose
heart was turned to ice...

The Twelve
Dancing Princesses

Anne Fine
Illustrated by Debi Gliori

Once upon a time there were twelve princesses,
and no one knew why their shoes were full
of holes...

Grey Wolf, Prince Jack and the Firebird

Alan Garner

Illustrated by James Mayhew

Once upon a time there was a prince who set out
to seek the mysterious firebird…

Mossycoat

Philip Pullman

Illustrated by Peter Bailey

Once upon a time there was a beautiful girl whose
mother made her a magical, mossy coat…

Cockadoodle-doo, Mr Sultana!

Michael Morpurgo
Illustrated by Michael Foreman

Once upon a time there was a rich and greedy
sultan who met a clever little cockerel...

Rapunzel

Jacqueline Wilson
Illustrated by Nick Sharratt

Once upon a time there was a baby who was
stolen by a witch...

The Six Swan Brothers

Adèle Geras
Illustrated by Ian Beck

Once upon a time there was a brave princess
who saw her six brothers turned into swans…

The Three Heads
in the Well

Susan Gates
Illustrated by Sue Heap

Once upon a time there were two stepsisters —
one good, one bad — who both went out to seek
their fortunes…

Rumpelstiltskin

Kit Wright
Illustrated by Ted Dewan

Once upon a time there was a beautiful girl who
would die if she couldn't spin straw into gold...

The Goose Girl

Gillian Cross
Illustrated by Jason Cockcroft

Once upon a time there was a princess who lost
everything she had ever owned...

The Pied Piper

K M Peyton
Illustrated by Victor Ambrus

Once upon a time there was a town infested
with a plague of horrible rats...

Puss in Boots

Diana Wynne Jones
Illustrated by Fangorn

Once upon a time there was a handsome miller's
son who owned a very clever cat...